CHRISTMAS
IN EXETER STREET

Diana Hendry *illustrated by* John Lawrence

WALKER BOOKS
AND SUBSIDIARIES
LONDON • BOSTON • SYDNEY

First published in Great Britain 1989
by Julia MacRae Books

This edition published 2002 by Walker Books Ltd
87 Vauxhall Walk, London SE11 5HJ

2 4 6 8 10 9 7 5 3 1

Text © 1989 Diana Hendry
Illustrations © 1989 John Lawrence

The right of Diana Hendry and John Lawrence to be identified as author
and illustrator respectively of this work has been asserted by them in accordance
with the Copyright, Designs and Patents Act 1988

This book has been typeset in Times

Printed in China

British Library Cataloguing in Publication Data:
a catalogue record for this book is available from the British Library

ISBN 0-7445-9417-0

The day before Christmas Eve, Ben and Jane's grandma and grandpa came to stay at the house in Exeter Street.
It was a lovely old house with big friendly windows, a holly wreath on the front door, and three chimney pots shaped like the crowns of the three wise men.

Grandpa George was a tall old sailor who came in his sea boots.
Grandma Ginny came with her knitting and her three cats, One, Two
and Three. Wherever Grandma Ginny went her knitting needles went in
and out under her elbows and One, Two and Three followed along behind
her. Grandpa George and Grandma Ginny brought a Christmas tree.

Ben and Jane's mother, Mrs Maggie Mistletoe, showed Grandpa George and Grandma Ginny where they were to sleep. She had given them the best spare bedroom. This had a big four-poster bed in it. Grandpa George parked his sea boots underneath it and the three cats jumped onto the bed and curled up together.

Ben and Jane's other grandma and grandpa also came to the house
in Exeter Street. They were small and skinny and wore their best hats,
a woolly bobble hat for Grandpa Angus and a beret with stars on it
for Grandma Fanny. Grandma Fanny brought a jar of her special
cranberry jelly.

Grandpa Angus and Grandma Fanny were given the second-best spare bedroom. This had a small iron bedstead in it. Grandma Fanny said "This bed is just the right size for two skinnies like us, we can snuggle up together." Grandpa Angus hung his bobble hat on one knob of the bed and Grandma Fanny hung her star-spangled beret on the other knob of the bed.

Ben and Jane's friends – Amelia, Annie and Amos – arrived on
Christmas Eve. Their parents had gone to Timbuktu on Very Important
Business and so they came to spend Christmas at the house in Exeter
Street. Amelia brought a basket of presents, Annie brought a big
Christmas pudding and Amos, who was only three, brought his cuddly
blanket and it trailed along behind him like a long, long tail.

Mrs Mistletoe took Amelia, Annie and Amos up the stairs to the attic. There they found five beds. Two bunk beds (one for Ben and one for Amos), two mattresses-on-the-floor (for Jane and Annie) and one camp bed with wobbly legs (for Amelia). "Mind you all hang up your Christmas stockings," said Mrs Mistletoe. Amos climbed up and down the ladder to the top bunk, trailing his blankie behind him.

Just after supper an unexpected uncle arrived. It was Uncle Bartholomew
back from Australia! Mrs Mistletoe made up a bed for him on the sofa
in front of the fire. This was just right for Uncle Bartholomew.

Because it had been very hot in Australia he was feeling very chilly; he was so cold he couldn't take off his mittens. Uncle Bartholomew brought a great box of Australian Delight (which was like Turkish Delight, only nicer).

The next to arrive was Mrs Mistletoe's friend Lily, who had nowhere
to live. And with Lily came Lily's baby, Lily-Lou. Lily slept on the small
sofa in the playroom which had been bounced on so often it was a very
funny sagging shape. But this didn't matter because so was Lily. Lily
brought home-made Christmas hats, each with a star glued on the front.

The kitchen sink was dried out very carefully, then lined with blankets, and Lily-Lou slept in there. Mrs Mistletoe hung Lily-Lou's stocking over the tap. Lily-Lou brought her smile.

Christmas Eve was very stormy and the vicar's roof blew off, so he and his wife and their four children all came to the house in Exeter Street. "Is there any room in the inn?" asked the vicar, and Mrs Mistletoe said yes, there was. "We've brought you a carol," said the vicar and they all stood on the doorstep and sang 'Away in a Manger'.

A bed was made up for the vicar and his wife in the bath and a lot of cushions were piled up in the corridor for the four children.

By this time there was quite a lot of noise in the house in Exeter Street and the children next door – Thomas, Tessa and Timothy – came to join the party.

They came in their pyjamas and they brought their sleeping bags and their Christmas stockings and they made a camp in the study.

At nine o'clock five aunts came from Abingdon bringing with them a big turkey and their three Pekinese dogs.

The aunts – Catherine, Clara, Christabel, Clothilda and Christiana – were very thin ladies so each of them was given a shelf on the dresser in the kitchen and tucked up tightly between the plates and the dangling cups.

The Pekinese dogs were packed into shopping baskets and tucked in with dolls' blankets kindly provided by Jane.

At midnight two fat men knocked at the door and asked for a bed for the night because their car had broken down. Each was given a mantelpiece. The first fat man said, "Please can our wives come in and we will all squash up together on the mantelpiece?"

But the wives were very fat, too, and Mrs Mistletoe said she didn't really think two people could fit on one mantelpiece.

"I have two large window-sills to spare," she said, "would you like to curl up there?" And the wives said yes please and was there a corner for their five children who were still in the car?

Mrs Mistletoe gave a small sigh and said that if Jane and Annie came into her bed, then the five children could sleep on the two mattresses in the attic. The car-children brought an enormous box of crackers.

Dear Father Christmas,

There are 18 children here. Please don't forget anyone —

love,
Maggie Mistletoe

P.S. Lily-Lou is in the kitchen sink.

When everyone was safely tucked up in bed, Mrs Mistletoe counted the number of children asleep in the house in Exeter Street and then she wrote a note for Father Christmas and pinned it on the front door.

No sooner had Mrs Mistletoe got into bed with Jane and Annie than she heard the sound of crying at the front door. She crept down the stairs and looked outside. There on the mat was a small black cat. He brought his snow-white paws. The small black cat slipped inside and found the room where Uncle Bartholomew was asleep on the sofa, dreaming about kangaroos. The small black cat sniffed Uncle Bartholomew and curled up at his feet.

The last person to arrive at the house in Exeter Street had a lot of trouble with his arithmetic. Father Christmas had to take off his boots and count on his toes to make sure he had remembered all eighteen children. And he had. (Even Lily-Lou.)

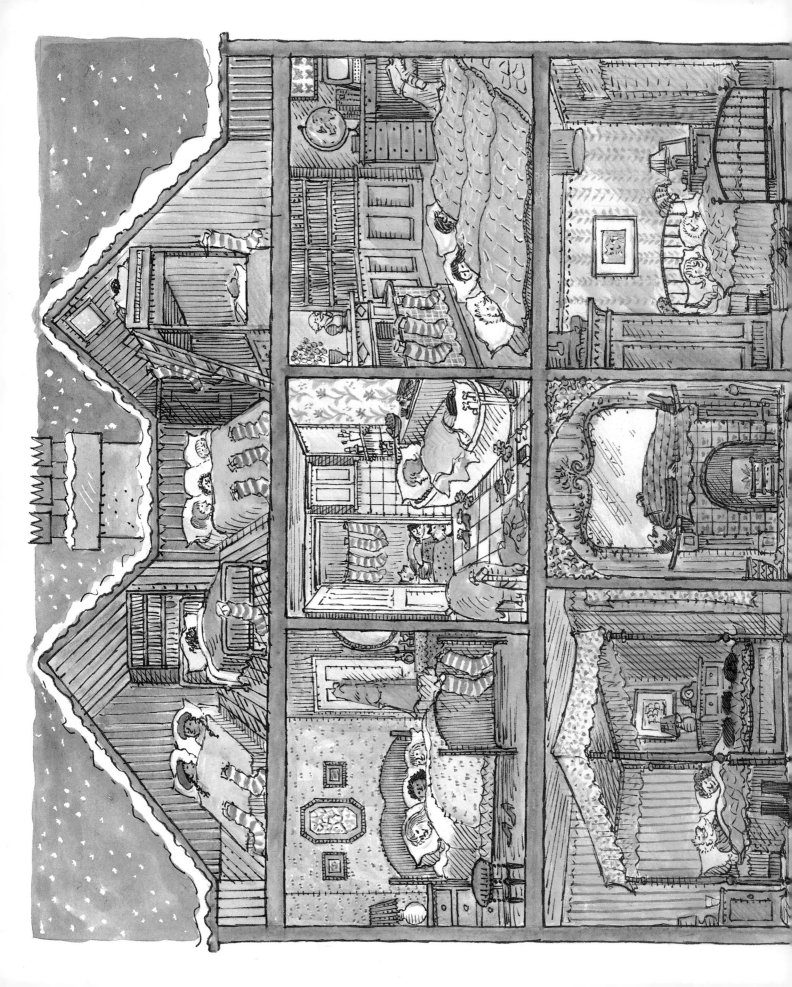

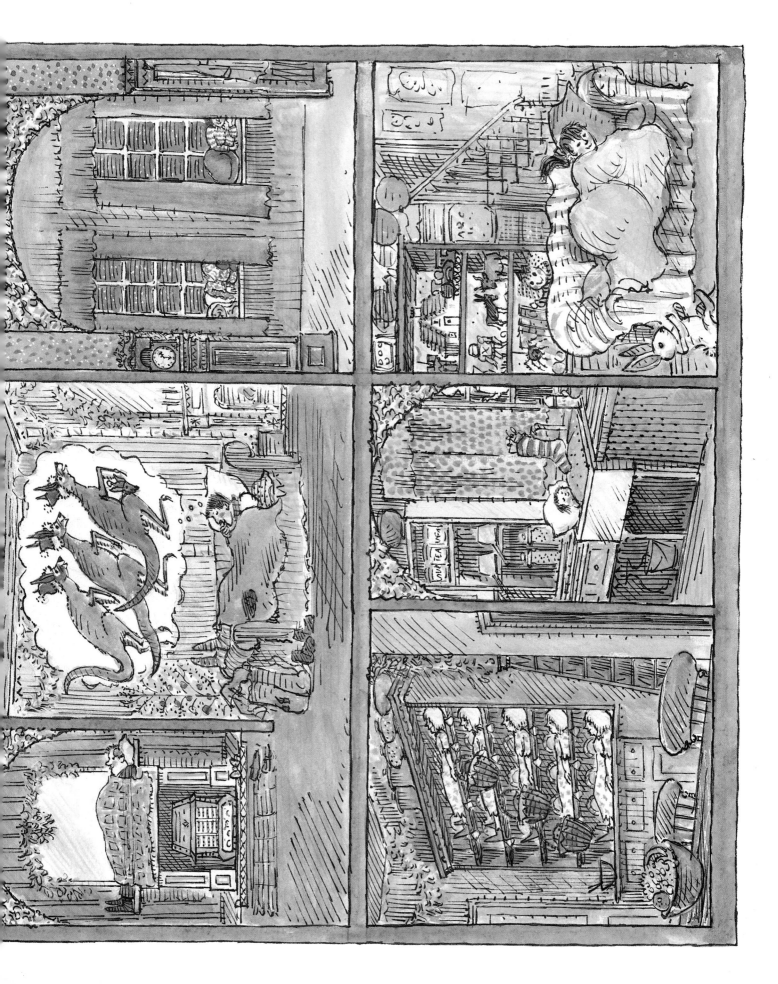

On Christmas Day morning they took Lily-Lou out of the sink and Mrs Mistletoe and Jane and Grandpa George peeled a whole sack of potatoes and then they all had a splendid Christmas dinner. They ate the Abingdon aunts' turkey with Grandma Fanny's cranberry jelly and afterwards they had Annie's Christmas pudding.

They all wore Lily's Christmas hats (except for Amos who wore his blankie tied round his head because he felt happiest that way) and they pulled the car-children's crackers. When dinner was over they sat round the fire and ate Uncle Bartholomew's Australian Delight and it was like eating sunshine.

Everyone agreed that the house in Exeter Street was the best place of all to be at Christmas time. The little black cat, curled up in Mrs Mistletoe's lap, thought he might stay until next Christmas and Lily-Lou, snuggled up in Uncle Bartholomew's arms, waved her little curly fingers at the Christmas tree and smiled and smiled and smiled.